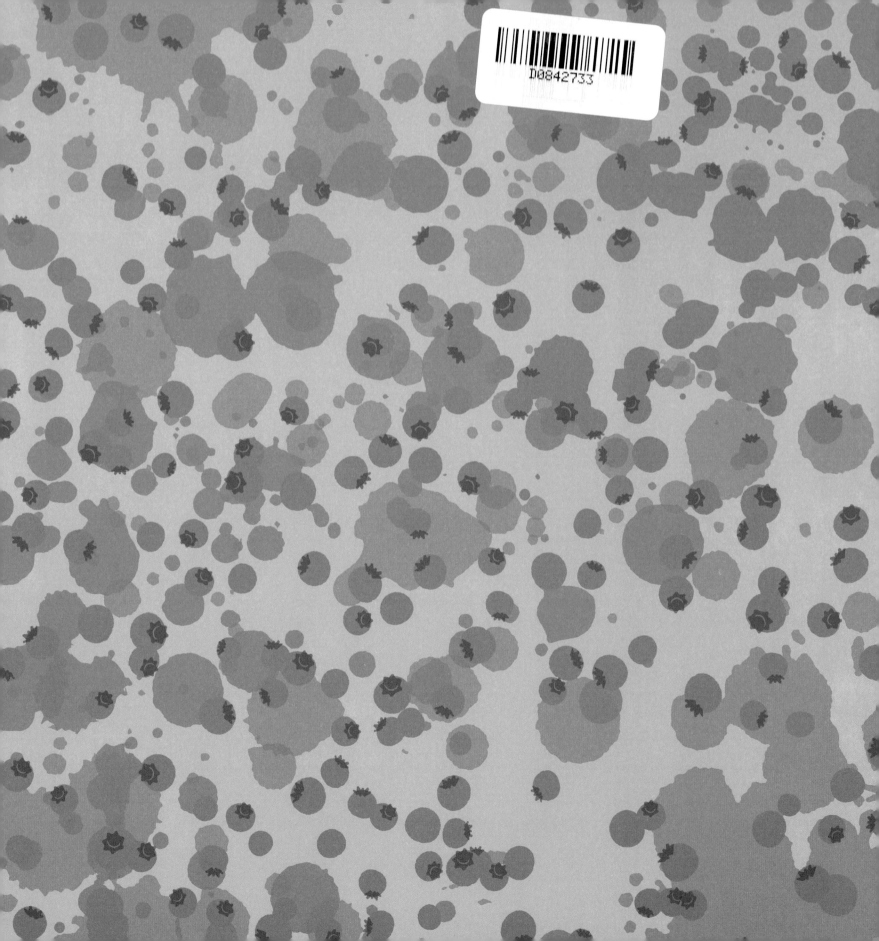

BLUE BADGER
AND THE BIG BREAKFAST

happy yak

To be without some of the things you want
is an indispensible part of happiness.
—Bertrand Russell

For Mick and Amelie—Huw
For Julian and Karl—Ben

Brimming with creative inspiration, how-to projects, and useful information to enrich your everyday life, quarto.com is a favorite destination for those pursuing their interests and passions.

© 2022 Quarto Publishing Group USA Inc.
Text © 2022 Huw Lewis Jones
Illustrations © 2022 Ben Sanders

Huw Lewis Jones has asserted his right to be identified as the author of this work.
Ben Sanders has asserted his right to be identified as the illustrator of this work.

First published in 2022 by Happy Yak, an imprint of The Quarto Group.
100 Cummings Center, Suite 265D, Beverly, MA 01915, USA.
T (978) 282-9590 F (978) 283-2742
www.quarto.com

A CIP record for this book is available from the Library of Congress.

ISBN: 978-0-7112-6757-2

Manufactured in Guangdong, China CC052022
9 8 7 6 5 4 3 2 1

MIX
Paper from
responsible sources
FSC
www.fsc.org
FSC® C008047

BLUE BADGER
AND THE BIG BREAKFAST

Huw Lewis Jones & Ben Sanders

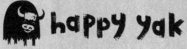
happy yak

It's breakfast time.
Life is sweet.
Badger has so much to eat.

Blue berries.
My favorite.

Morning, Badger.
How's things?
It looks like you're having a nice big breakfast.

Yes, thanks.

Are you playing with your friends today?

Nope.
I'm pretty busy.
Got lots of eating to do.

Hello, Badger.
Something smells good.
Berries for breakfast again.
Lucky you.

Have you seen Dog?

Not yet.
I'm still pretty busy.
So much to eat.

Oh hey, Dog.
How's life?

I've lost something.
Sorry, can't stop.
I have to find it...

Find what?

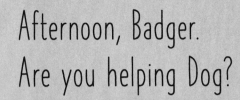

Afternoon, Badger.
Are you helping Dog?

Not yet.
Should I be?
I'm still eating.

Dog has lost his favorite ball.
Have you seen it?

I don't think I've seen it.
Have I?

Don't worry, Badger.
Look deep inside yourself
for the answers.

It was a **blue** ball, wasn't it?

Owl, what should I do?
I think I ate it.

Well. It's simple. Worrying gets you nowhere.
The storm will pass. The early bird catches the worm.
We all make mistakes. The best things in life aren't things.
True friends are all you really need. In giving back, we receive.
Patience is a virtue. And, happiness comes from within.

Huh?
I don't get it.

Just relax, Badger.
Go find Dog.

Hey, Dog.
Want to play fetch?

Oh hello, Badger.
I'm sorry.
I can't find my
ball anywhere.

Um. About that.
It's me that should
be sorry. I think
I might have eaten it.

But you know what, Dog.
We don't need a ball to play...

...we've got berries!

And we've got...

...each other!

That was fun.
I'm really sorry about your ball.

Don't worry, Badger.
Maybe it'll turn up...

...someday.